SAIL AWAY

Donald Crews

94 94

Greenwillow Books / New York

To the <u>Seabiscuit</u>,
captain and crew,
and to being here
to tell this tale

The full-color illustrations were created
with Dr. Martin's Concentrated Water Colors
applied with brush and airbrush. The text
type is Akzidenz Grotesk Bold Italic.

a division of William Morrow
& Company, Inc.,
1350 Avenue of the Americas,
New York, NY 10019.
Printed in Singapore
by Tien Wah Press
First Edition
10 9 8 7 6 5 4 3 2 1

Library of Congress
Cataloging-in-Publication Data

Crews, Donald.
Sail away / by Donald Crews.
p. cm.
Summary: A family takes an
enjoyable trip in their sailboat
and watches the weather
change throughout the day.
ISBN 0-688-11053-3 (trade).
ISBN 0-688-11054-1 (lib. bdg.)
[1. Sailing–Fiction.]
I. Title. PZ7.C8682Sai
1995 [E]–dc20 94-6004
CIP AC

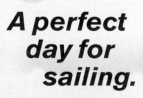

A perfect day for sailing.

*We row the dinghy
out to our sailboat.*

**Everything ready,
we motor from our mooring.**
p u t t ... p u t t ... p u t t ...

putt...putt...putt...
Under the bridge.
putt...putt...putt...

putt...putt...putt...
Past the lighthouse.
Motor off. *putt...* **Sails up ...**

Wind's up...

**Sail away
through the day.**

**Sailing, sailing.
Clear skies turn
cloudy and gray.**

**Gray skies darken.
Seas swell.**

Darker skies,
higher seas...
**Angry
seas.**
"Shorten sails!"

Sails down, we turn for home.

**Calm again at last.
The sun is setting
    as we motor toward port.**
p u t t . . . p u t t . . . p u t t . . .

putt...putt...putt...
Past the lighthouse.
putt...putt...putt...

putt...putt...putt...
Under the bridge.
putt...putt...putt...

Moored!